PINWHEEL

BookSquirrel Publications

BookSquirrel Publication

Mahadev Totala Nager, Indore (M.P),452001
Regd Under MSME
Website:
www.booksquirrelpublication.com

"PINWHEEL"

By: Aarthi Sampath

ISBN: 978-93-89923-90-2

English Anthology

Book Formatting: Rubal Choudhary

Cover Design: Ronak Chavda

<u>DISCLAMER</u>

This Anthology is a work of fiction. The writers have tried to make sure that all the Write-ups in this book are original, and plagiarism free.

All the write-ups in this book are unique, and they belong solely to the Co-Authors.

In case of any detection of Plagiarism, neither the publishing house, nor the compiler is to be held responsible.

The sole responsibilities of the Write-ups are on that writer.

ACKNOWLEDGEMENT

All Praises to the Almighty for believing in me,

I am thankful Rubal Choudhary and **Booksquirrel Publications** for giving this wonderful Anthology **"PINWHEEL"** without whom this project would not be possible.

And I thank my Contributing authors who gave their Amazing pieces, and to my readers and everyone who'vemade me to write to seek purpose of my existence.

<u>AARTHI SAMPATH</u>

I am Aarthi Sampath, Artist based in Chennai India, 38 yrs. old, with Muscular Dystrophy, using wheelchair, I have written articles about me,asI'mconstantly judged for my physical adversity.
I have Co-Authored 40+ Anthologies

And also compiling anthologies

My Insta Id: @aarthisampath_

<u>PINWHEEL</u>

the cold sun glowed
With tiny crumbs of hope,
Peeling the frozen season,
and Letting the wind blow,
to gently Drift the weight of unsaid love
off our tongues,
we rose on the horizon
Stretching colours of faith
as the season watched us
Unfurl,
the pinwheel spun a tune without words,
For us to listen before we go.
For us to sing along
For us to swirl, and
only for us.

PINWHEEL

<u>RUBAL CHOUDHARY</u>

<u>Quote</u> –

Believing in yourself has been the first priority for the
ones who have been hurted many a times.
There's always a good or a bad outcome of success, but
by believing in yourself in helps you to reach heights.

PINWHEEL

ATEETY MUSKAN KUJUR

It was unlike any other day...
I saw the clouds pouring its heart today!
Season of love it was...
The Season of Spring it was!
The time when the loved ones would pour their heart out,
I saw the Sky crying out!!!
I felt heavy that day.
Nothing! I could do but to pray!
The feeling was engrossing me...
Hovering around my head like a busy bee.
Hoped the best for the Next Day.
But who knew it would be pouring like "That" day
It is unlike any other day...
For you are not with me Today!

PINWHEEL

<u>NEHA</u>

I was that morning dew
Which is pure to the core.
But I never got the recognition.

I was that innocent wince of a little kid.
Which doesn't really have a valid purpose.
But I got labelled for it.

Now
I am the wild winds of the West.
That destroys everything in its path.
But I am called conservative now.

This is the world that works in reverse.

It calls,
Pure as fake.
Sees,
Innocence as plotting.
Brands,
Arrogance as eminent.

Welcome to the dire truth of 21st century.

PINWHEEL

<u>NISHA KATTIKULAM</u>

QUOTE 1:

You will be in my dark, and in my light.
In my credence and my twilight
I will praise you in my story and my anthem
In my poetry and my poem.

QUOTE 2:

Sometimes, it's only writing where I find Solace.
After all the rush and hustle, when I return to my dome.
I sit in my comfort space, feel complete and home.
For my pen offers me peace, and my book keeps me at ease.

PINWHEEL

<u>SHREESH VERMA</u>

And when I look into those eyes,
Even if they are not at me.
I see something in them,
What the world can't see.
You don't say a word,
I talk for hours to you.
Yes, you are beautiful,
My mom says that too.
What gets into me at your sight?
I feel like trapped in mazes.
Why can't I say a word of what,
I've talked to your images.

PINWHEEL

MEENAKSHI PERIYASAMY

PERMANENCE OF NOTHING

Ink dried to make words last
Last line of lyrics stuck in mind
Mind backlogged in forgetting
Forgetting seemed harder than remembering

Foul memory frozen in dead past
Past stood in the mist of present
Present found bizarre future
Future invisible in trail of heart

Mirage played in moribund of love
Love felt loneliness at cliff of nothing
Nothing gave life sparks to everything
Everything becomes non-existent in circle.

PINWHEEL

SANTU CHOWDHURY

QUOTE 1:

Friendship is not about the right person!
But creating the right Relationships.
It's not, how much we care in the beginning!
But how much we care till the end.

QUOTE 2:

Our friendship has
become our "HABIT"!
Even if you take out 'H',
'abit' remains.
Take out A,
Still 'bit' remains.
Finally take out B,
Still 'it', remains...!

SUJITH RAMAN

LOVE YOURSELF

Do you want to love someone,
Someone special and not just anyone
Try to love the one in the mirror,
Cause he is best than the better
Look deep inside and you find the one,
You were searching in everyone
The one who understands you the most,
Like a guardian angel, like a ghost
With you to love and to fight,
To be with you in your wrong and right
To live with you in your low and high,
To tell you not only all truth, but also lie
So, why don't you try the one in mirror,
To be with you, in cold when you shiver
In love, you will see your own beauty,
And you will never yourself pity
A happy soul will then spread love,
Even the toughest in front of you will bow...

PINWHEEL

SEMINA FIROZBHAI HIMANI

QUOTE 1:

Life can be exactly how we want it to be if you Stop
comparing yourself with others, try to satisfy with what you
have, and never give up on failure.

QUOTE 2:

I have always looked up to you now it's time to do something
different and unique by which my parents will proud on me
and can say to whole world proudly it's my daughter.

SUPRIT BAGWALE

DEAR STRANGER

Scrolling my Insta,
Exists a starry.
She looks attractive,
Something distractive.

One thing is common,
We both are stranger.
She is not the last,
But she is the least.

We don't know,
What's our relation.
Just one thing is there,
Something is near.

There was something special,
But We both are prestigious.
She was busy all the time,
and I disrupt her every time.

PINWHEEL

MANSHI AGGARWAL

QUOTE 1:

I kissed the wall with a heavy heart and tears rolling down my
cheeks
today, was the last day of three beautiful years of my life.

QUOTE 2:

I had lost faith in love that night when u slept knowing I was
crying!

PINWHEEL

<u>DR SHALAKHA BHIMJIYANI</u>

The day I first met you
You said you would never fall in love
Now that we get each other
Don't you feel any different?

We are two opposite poles
But baby together we are best
When will you realise
That I am not like rest!

There's only one life
No time to wait, to waste
I know you have been hurt before
Baby let me ease your ache

Together we can have it all
Baby please hold my hand tight
There's no turning back now
You lying by my side feels so right!

PINWHEEL

<u>POOJA SHARMA</u>

QUOTE 1:

Everyone brings their own music with them,
Sometimes it's soft as a melody and
Sometimes it wakes us up with the sound of rocking drums.

QUOTE 2:

Disconnected from the stars,
we've landed here,
merging threads of lives.

PINWHEEL

ELAKKIYA SRUTHI

QUOTE 1:

Rose
The Queen of flowers
Suicides gradually because of it's
Tremendous jealousy towards you...

To the prettiest girl in my world......

QUOTE 2:

One day will make you
Understand me!!
You will realize the sense of my pain
That day you die to live with me
When I already died....

PINWHEEL

<u>SUBHASINI BALAN</u>

QUOTE 1:

LOVE >> FRIENDSHIP

"People say,
Love breaks the heart;
On the contrary,
Friendship mends it with the same Love.'"

QUOTE 2:

NOW & THEN

Let the 'Past' be the passing clouds,
Celebrate the 'Presence',
Let the 'Future' be the flying colours.

DHEEPA SARAVANAN

PAPER BOATS

Made with dailies, by little hands
Paused under the roof, for rain's departure;
By descrying at all these,
Rain faded by shedding its last drop
With a group of captains
Cruises are ready for a short voyage
Even though you know,
You'll get drowned at any moment
Sailed by spreading your wings,
Like no one can't seize me
Created sparkles in that minuscule gap;
Like you floated on the drained water,
Smile floats on the lips of the little faces

PINWHEEL

HARSHITA CHAURASIA

QUOTE 1:

My heart sets with the sun,
When the time comes for us to take leave.
Why can't we delay this separation?
Atleast until the stars get busy forming a new constellation.

QUOTE 2:

I loved her; she knew.
She knew, I was losing hope too.
Hope too, came back.
Came back, when she loved back.

<u>JAY PATEL</u>

The Lost Sunshine

There is this burning rage infinitely infinite diffused here in
the core,
Actually, I'm more confused, empty and lonely. Those
unfathomable depths were entirely unaccountable, what's
more reciting is clinging to you for love.
The pity bounded devils inside coalescing fixation. When all
the charges will pause, I want you to feel the benumbed
strings of love. Until then, let me get closer, closer to finding a
way between haunted memories and uncertainty of your eyes!

PINWHEEL

SHIVANI PRIYANGA

It had been a long day
You cared me!
It had been a long day
You admired and teased me!
It had been a long day
You fought with me!
It had been a long day
You argued with me!
It had been a long day
You compromised me!
It had been a long day
You talked with me over nights!
It had been a long day
You said "love you"!
And babe Do you know one thing?
It had been a long day
I have practiced to it...

<u>SOWMYA REDDY</u>

LOVE ME
Love me like the stars
For they stay up all night for the Moon, with the Moon
For they stay up all night waiting for the Moon's arrival after
every fortnight
For they stay up all night at times of the Moon's transition
For they stay up all night accompanying the Moon
For they stay up all night forming intricate caricatures which
leave us to our own imagination
For they stay up all night decorating the sky
For they stay up all night twinkling endlessly, never lessening
their shine and even strengthening the Moon
For they stay up all night for you me and all
So, if you are to love me then do so like the stars.

PINWHEEL

U.S.VIDISHA

I don't want mornings,
I love dancing alone to the tune of the night.
I'm sorry I don't need the freedom you give me, the freedom
of a kite.
No, I don't have to shine bright always,
For what's the use of such sheen that blinds you to see the real
me,
behind my fake smile.
I don't need your hand let me drown,
Let me discover myself in the soulful sombreness.
I'm sorry I don't want to bloom,
I'm cosy here in my little bud, safe from the world's gloom.
I'm sorry I can't fly, I wasn't taught to,
Just laughed at.
But I can walk,
So sorry I'll be a little late.
But I'm no more sorry for it.

PINWHEEL

<u>SAMBARDHANA DIKSHIT</u>

QUOTE 1:

I wish to live in peace
but the life offers me to live on pieces.

QUOTE 1:

It's not that someone between us is wrong or right
We need to sort out it but why always we ended up with a
fight
You choose to be silent
while my inner voice goes violent ...

<u>MEENU MINOCHA</u>

QUOTE 1:

A million wounds have I
mute witnesses to your borrowed glory...
If each spake a lyrical verse
withered would be your derived story!

QUOTE 1:

I used to think
that the stars were so far away ....
until I met you and found them
nestled in your eyes!

DEEPA DASH

MYSELF...!

Summers often welcome winter,
Water even flows out of drain,
Same is the deal in life,
Some are rich but some strive.

The happiness in life can never be found,
If we search it under the ground.
We are made of dust and will return to dust,
But meanwhile let not our life burst...!

Happiness and peace is what we need.
To fulfil each and every deed.
Choose an option of being happy?
I would choose "myself...!"

MAONGKABA JAMIR

Wallflower

Even with the walls built high around yourself,
Your mind still so loud.
Maybe you're a secret to the world
Maybe a code to be deciphered carefully
Maybe a wallflower
Seeking sweet solitude.
Let me not disrupt your peace
But you have instilled in me
An interest in your awkward silence.
So, tell me -
Of your daydreams,
Of your fantasies, hidden behind
That timid smile,
Of things that exhaust you
Of things that delight you
Of stories behind the subtle hellos.
Tell me more
Tell me more about you.

PINWHEEL

<u>TANU KAPOOR</u>

A person who can read,
Nuances of your thoughts, emotions
And desire is more rare,
But we have yet to meet a person,
Who doesn't say that is precisely what;
He/she is looking for,
Rare is not the same as imaginary,
And imaginary doesn't exist.

QUOTE 1:

Until you embrace the pain of your growth, you'll remain
stuck in your present situations; You must embrace the
uncomfortable parts of life to evolve.

PINWHEEL

<u>MADHURI BHADRA</u>

QUOTE 1:

SMILE
You told me that smiling helps to brighten the day,
Today we met again and you smiled and I thought you were
right.

QUOTE 2:

LOST WOLF
A wolf lost his tracks from his pack,
Roaming around searching but deep forest holding him back,
Came across a dark cave thinking of taking rest,
Got up next day searching and howling in attempt of hearing
howls back.

PINWHEEL

<u>ANUSHA WAGHADHARE</u>

QUOTE 1:

Don't you take Life seriously.
It's just a nightmare.
One day we shall awaken to death...
And everything shall fall in place...

QUOTE 2:

At times one trespasses a body,
Not the Soul.
Virgin is such Soul,
Till eternity.

PINWHEEL

DR. TILAK DIXIT

QUOTE:

There was an art in his creation
That was THROWN by the nation
Rain vanished the fancy
Which was THRONE by the nation

PINWHEEL

<u>JILL SHAH</u>

QUOTE 1:

Only when you know it CAN happen,
Only then it happens to exists
And Only then,
It betides to become existence.

QUOTE 2:

Ensnared into delusion, attachment rose.
Withering the karma,
Carcass stands tainted
And so, becomes the soul...

PINWHEEL

SAURABH

QUOTE 1:

We know the truth,
we justify only the lies!

QUOTE 2:

We profoundly had dead flowers,
to mark the beginning of love!

PINWHEEL

<u>POORVI SINGHAL</u>

QUOTE 1:

"Authority was the only injunction he now complied to. She gloomed for; the man she had once conquered had turned into a serf."

QUOTE 2:

"When agitated, I cry. Neither when elated, am I dry. Sobbing is an expression."

PINWHEEL

<u>RUSHVEEN K UBAN</u>

QUOTE 1:

You're slipping through my fingers
even though I've been holding you firmly
please don't leave yet
I wanna hold you more tightly.

QUOTE 2:

And when he left,
he asked me to do the most difficult thing
he asked me to,
stay happy.

<u>TANUPREET KAUR</u>

REALITY CHECK

Two sides of the same coin,
personifies the real life.

Some can be your tears,
some can be laughter.
Some can be your disturbance,
some can be relief.
Some can be your rejection,
some can be acceptance.
Some can be your mess,
some can be peace.
Some can be your cold,
some can be warmth.
Some can be your hell,
some can be heaven.

Swinging on this seesaw,
brings us back to the real life.

PINWHEEL

SHARMILA ROSE

QUOTE 1:

MIND TO HEART:

Please give some time to sleep
Without your memories.

QUOTE 2:

The Beauty of the loneliness:
That is my tears said
To my lips to SMILE

SIMARDEEP SINGH GANDHI

DEFINITION OF LOVE

'I am a veracious lover'
is what everyone claims.
The consequence of mishap with one of two,
zaps the relationship in a go.

At times, the case is different.
It might be of getting affronted.
The so called 'relationship',
sinks in the ocean after falling from the ship.

Oh people, when will you learn the meaning?
True love isn't a feeling,
among two bodies, it is a sensation,
among two souls...

<u>FATEMA. ALIASGAR. AKOLAWALA</u>

THE MOON

The moon is half
Just like my heart
A dimly shining armour
In the night of the dark

The depressions of loneliness
The creases of parting
Mournful sighs being unheard
Inner beauty losing its shine

Bearing the flag of victory
Why is the heart losing from the mind?
Just like the moon
Turning deaf and blind!

PINWHEEL

UMA SHAKTHI

QUOTE 1:

All of us are on a journey towards one destination...
That is
CEMETERY...

QUOTE 2:

When I look at my hands
I remember that it was holder by
Your hands once upon a time...

PINWHEEL

<u>KARUNASRI GOVINDA RAO LABBA</u>

I met you as a stranger, then took you as my friend.
Our friendship is something that will never end.
When I was in darkness that needed some light,
You came to me and hugged me tight.

You took my hands and dried my tears.
You woke me up to end my fears.
You took my hand and made me see
That God has a special plan for me.

You helped me laugh when I was sad,
You made me tough when I felt bad.
You made me think when I got mad,
With you, this brainless kid is so glad.

Our friendship made me see the light.
Our friendship showed to me what was right.
I hope our friendship will never bend.
I hope our friendship will never end.

PINWHEEL

<u>POOJA PANDIT</u>

QUOTE 1:

Life is full of hardships
It depends on us how we live,
With a Smile on our face,
Or with a Frowning look.

QUOTE 2:

Having Long Distance, Doesn't Matter
Having Long Conversation, Doesn't Matter
Sharing your Feelings every day, Doesn't Matter
Still One can be Connected to their loved Ones,
All you need is to LOVE.

PINWHEEL

<u>SHEETAL DUBEY</u>

"SHE'S TIRED"

She's tired,
Tired of all...

Her mind was gripped by an unwanted force,
Her heart was ripped off from its core.

The pain was hard to endure,
But she did it till she can cure.

Now she's tired,
Tired to say it hurts no more.

Let her go,
Go where she wants,

She's hurting,
Hurting her own demons.

But she realized,
Realized a little too late
Her demons are her own self.

PINWHEEL

<u>RAKSHITA NAIN</u>

QUOTE 1:

It was beautiful as a rainbow,
The moist and warm relationship,
Did not we know already,
It disappears as the weather change.

QUOTE 2:

We are stuck at the materialistic,
What matters are actions,
What precedes them are words,
But what makes it happen is our belief.

PINWHEEL

ANIRUDH MALYALA

Your words are made of musical essence,
Please sing to me, so I can hear the world faultlessly.!
This aroma of yours is so pure,
Please come closer, so I can discover the pleasantness and
fragrance.!
Let our feelings and bodies hug,
So that I can feel the warmness and closeness of the true
world.!
Now, bury that forehead of yours on my chest,
So, I'll forever share my heart with you.!
Breathe into me when our lips fights,
So, the aftermath will make me whole.!
& You! From the depths of my heart,
I'll share myself, my love and desire!!

PINWHEEL

DIVYA KHANNA

QUOTE 1:

You are more of what they can't see,
It's okay to not let them know,
And let them be a fluke.

QUOTE 2:

You lost me,
I lost my world,
You never realized but,
You stayed my only world.

PINWHEEL

ANJANI

QUOTE 1:

Never underestimate the ever-smiling people. They know how
to survive blood moments. They create their own world and
fill it with happiness. They are damn dangerous I say!

QUOTE 2:

Knowing to sprout, shouldn't feel a little low for being buried.

PRIYAMBDA ARYA

When you stand next to me

I feel like a tree is beside me
That makes me what i want to be
I feel very real what I am exactly
You make me happy very gently
A relation between us that
No one can understand
You give me strength to set myself
That's why I call you my soulmate

QUOTE:

If I can go back in time through photographs

Take people back there
Who have forgotten
What they were and
What they became

GAREEMA RAJU

GROWING UP

Growing up is all about,
Reminiscing the past mistakes,
And avoiding their repetition,
Reliving the old memories,
And re-establishing the old relations,
Forgoing the immaturity and becoming a mature and a
practical person.

Love

If love had an address,
It would be resplendent with mesmerizing gardens of
blooming emotion,
And filled with extravagant rooms filled with exuberant
romance and ardent passion,
It would bear the likeness of heaven,
And only allow the entry of souls filled with virtuous love and
devotion.

PINWHEEL

KHUSHBOO MITTAL

QUOTE 1:

The leaves that
has fallen now,
Once made the tree
feel alive

QUOTE 2:
Let me embellish your scars,
So, they will shine too

<u>ABHIPSA KAR</u>

SOMBER NOON
Caught in the spree of a thousand eyes,
Landed her in a dilemma of thoughts,
Atmosphere around her turned dark,
Witnessing hundreds of lightening sparks.

Questions of the league, that remained unanswered,
Left her emotions haunted by scars of the past,
Lying on the floor, she screamed for help,
Yet, nobody noticed her yelp.

Excruciated, she sought for vengeance,
From the sinner who ripped her apart.
The fire within heart, blazed like glittering gold,
Transformed her into a 'Phoenix of Justice' for avenging all
those demons in disguise of humans.

SOUBHAGYA R KATTI

ARCTIC TERN!
And the day had come,
To head back home,
Indeed, the Arctic's!

All I had to habituate to,
Along the changing-challenging weather-monsters on my
path;
Not because I ain't adored,
But cause I'll fit in where I belong;
Yes! I'm the gutsy Arctic Tern!

Retrospectives and flashbacks of adios;
To all my fellow birdy acquaintances,
To perpetuate the onset:
But what if I died in Sirocco?
C'mon I'm the valiant Arctic Tern!

What if hope ever abandons me?
Ah! To get back all the morality; I'd fight back beasts!
'Cause yeah, I'm the gallant Arctic Tern!

PINWHEEL

KAUSHIK DAS

QUOTE 1:

I always keep a bonfire of spring
burning in my heart
But your memories
always keep the winner awake

QUOTE 2:

The snow has covered up your garden today
Like u did
Covered up.
My Earth's sun with your sweat, last summer

PINWHEEL

SAKET SINGH

LOOKING IN VAIN FOR MEMORIES TO RAIN

At the deepest of shore
There are some chores
Looking in vain
Waiting for memories to rain.
Another wave passed by
He breathed a deep sigh
Some moments of past
Revised and will long last.
Sometimes unwanted pain
Of rightful memories that claim
Years passed but sorrows stay
Think then sad or cheerful play.
Confident future or past is shame
Time will fly, you act or lay
Time of choice other can't take
This is the risk you have to make
Stop lamenting, see a new day
Learn from the past and achieve the aim.

BHAVESH PARMAR

SLEEPLESS IN MUMBAI
It's another hectic day in fast, non-stop life in Mumbai
Robed in solitude, I lie on the bed awake at midnight
The crows crow undeterred by the serenity of the night
A cat stalks a pigeon on my balcony
The whistle of the watchman rises and falls
The harried traffic has calmed down,
though shadows still chase each other down the streets
The cool moon is busy dropping dew on the grass, while the
stars shine white
Even the dreams have deserted me tonight
The dark is almost gone, the stars are about to set
The cuckoo takes over from the crow and the rooster awakens

Yet! another day welcomes, yet! another sleepless night in
Mumbai
It's time to get up and rush for work.

PINWHEEL

PRACHITA ARORA

QUOTE:
A big fat room
With big dreams,
Some were part of setbacks,
Some were because of parent's restriction,
And some just found good in that!

PINWHEEL

<u>AMOHA</u>

QUOTE 1:

You don't have the best life but let the people stay in this
confusion that you have

QUOTE 2:

No one has decided to stay always, so let our smile decide to
stay

PINWHEEL

<u>RITIKA WADHWA</u>

It's not only you, Not me, It's us
Who didn't made it.
It's not only you, who wanted it to start
It's also me,who started it all together...
It's not only you, Loving me
It's also me, Loving you too.
It's not only you,who lied many times
It's also me,who didn't understand you're lying...
It's not only you,who didn't understand my love for you
It's also me,who can't make you realize my worth...
It's not only about me,who trusted all your words
It's also about you,who broke that trust ...
It's not only me,who didn't tried to make it happen all again
It's also you,who never wanted it to happen all again...
It's not only you, Not me, It's us...
Who ourselves had losted
our own beautiful paradise...
Our own soothing sunsets...
Our own adoring us...

PINWHEEL

<u>RITESH SARKAR</u>

QUOTE 1:

She is the one, I understood
When her tears were the reason of my sadness
And her smile was the reason of my happiness

QUOTE 2:

"when was the last time you made your parents proud?"
someone asked
"Everyday! When they see boys of my age smoking and I am
not among them " I replied.

PINWHEEL

<u>SAKTHI GNANASUNDARAM</u>

QUOTE 1:

If people had carefully invested their time instead of money, they would have been billionaires by now.

QUOTE 2:

Just like biological system, even people come from different environments. It's not reasonable to expect everyone to behave alike at all situations.

ANJALI JHA

LIFE IN GRAVEYARD

Life is very peaceful in graveyard,
No one can tease you,
No one can hurt you,
The spirit of soul and whole body diffused in the soil,
Sometimes it turns into ashes,
Sometimes it putrefies along with soil,
Grabbing and absorbing the whole body goes into peace,
Body is made up of five things,
And finally, it is mixed up with these five things,
Your body, your soul is covered by leaves as well as sand, soil
and water,
But you have no heed,
You are sleeping peacefully,
No one can torture you now,
Now only graveyard is your friend,
Rain helps you to wash your body,
Leaves and soil helps you to cover your body,
Now you are living in your own world,
You are free from mess up world.

PINWHEEL

<u>NEHA LEKHAK</u>

times when I'm mishandled,
by this overthinking skill
thoughts that stray like shadows,
is it karma or is it guilt?
forbidden, to lay
barren, raw & stilt
provoked by situations,
burning within
they say, don't vent it out
you'd be judged,
obscene & forbade
all I did was,
listened to my heart once
I'm ashamed,
concluded & assessed
I've again fallen,
for the wrong deal

PINWHEEL

<u>SONI JAIN</u>

SHHH...YOU ARE A GIRL!
Keep your hair locks behind
Keep those rules in your mind,
Remove that spellbinding liner....
It may let them notice you more finer,

Those strapping eyes...
Tearing her groovy drape,
Darling, conceal your carcass....
But don't defy to speak out,
B'Coz shhh...you are a girl!

Hey slut!! The way they exhibit...
To those wearing the slinky sheath,
But hey!! Don't... don't even dare!
To utter the words, it's not fair...
Coz baby, shh...you are a girl!

She wants to fight...
To hold their neck tight,
Not having any option instead of being quiet,
B'Coz shh...she is a girl!

SAGARIKA PRIYADARSHANEE

NOSTALGIA

Whenever I stumble upon something belonging to my past, the memories associated with it are refreshed again. A sudden wave of varied emotions clutches me with its claws so tightly that sometimes I find myself teleported into the past reliving the incidents yet again.

Nostalgia hits me like a hurricane which swallows me whole and tosses me away into a deserted island.

PINWHEEL

<u>MUSKAAN GULATI</u>
<u>(TRARA)</u>

I WRITE FOR MYSELF

Writing gives me Pleasure,
Writing gives me Smile.
People read, People judge
Let them know
I WRITE FOR MYSELF.

Writing gives me Peace,
Writing changes my Mood.
People read, People Judge
Let them know
I WRITE FOR MYSELF.

Writing has the Power
which turns my Heavy heart and Teary Eyes to Shiny smiling
Face.
Let people read, Let People judge,
Just let them know
I WRITE FOR MYSELF.

PINWHEEL

<u>PON RANJANI S.B</u>

Mind: What have you done to him?
Heart: I have loved him
I have prayed for him
I have understood him
I have forgiven all his flaws
I have waited for him
I have longed and craved for him.
Mind: what will you do for him?
Heart: I will do all the above mentioned
Things in double triple manner...
I love him as He is!...
Mind: Aren't you mad doing these things?
Heart: yup! Exactly insane over Him!

PINWHEEL

PRAHARSHA ISRUPU

Quote 1:

Sometimes you become numb not because you don't want to react. Rather it's just because you feel yourself much mature to ignore the shit that disturbs your inner self.

Quote 2:

If you do not understand the other person it doesn't mean that they are wrong. It only means that you lack the ability to understand them.

PINWHEEL

MANDAR GAWAS

DREAMS

You are my lucid dreams,
The dream I knew would not come true,
As the moon in sky laughed at me,
For chasing behind some lucid dream...

You envy, you smile, you share,
When I'm with you.
But can you now hear me,
As i call you,
For you have someone,
With whom you laugh much often,
For now, I'm just a mere part of you.

It's time for me to move apart,
But I shall carry your memories as a souvenir,
I can't erase you,
More I try more it grows,
It's the love I one sidedly shared with you!!

PINWHEEL

SAMRIDDHI SRIVASTAVA

Ah! Let the love be true
Meeting of our souls under the sky blue
Holding of hands, eyes in eyes
Under the bright stars with glittering flies
In your arms let my life be,
Flowers will evolve you will see
Hearts full of happiness, let the love shine
No more crush, officially mine

SANJANA

MUSIC

When no one really wished to care
Music was indeed there
When nothing seems to heal my pain
The thought about music was mostly sane
When dark memories haunts
Music heals with no taunts
When gloom fills my heart
When my past tears me apart
Music helps me leave the pain behind
Music is the only one which is kind
In the world where everyone is a killer
Music is the only healer

PINWHEEL

<u>RIYA RASHMI DASH</u>

I wanted to thank you
But was unable to explain
What it means to have a friend
In sharing all life's joys and sorrows
It's good to know that our friendship
Is one of the endless devotions
Its patient, forgiving, never failing
When one's hand is with the other
It's ever faithful even when people condemn
And sparkles in the dark like gems
It does my heart good that you are just
An email away

Proof of a True Friend is knowing that if I were lost-You
would find me

PINWHEEL

VIRAT SHARMA

Though the moments we spent together were the most loved
one's but the memories now we sustain are the one's true in
their own way.
Her smile was my joy, her happiness was my priority but
somehow, we both were not in the same chapter for so long in
the book of destiny.
Sometimes we believe the love is all we need but there are
times where destiny is much more needed over love to make it
a reality.
It is not important to fall in love with the right person, it is
more important that you should fall in love with the right
person at right time also to make it happen.
Love has become a word these days, emotions have become
WhatsApp status, feelings have become stickers and
emoticons and loyalty has become a tattoo. Don't know where
are those days when all these together created the magical
bond between two souls

PINWHEEL

<u>HIMSHREE S</u>

We own powers,
We run positions,
But when life decides to twist things up,
Helpness governs our universe.

Still one can power through,
For the will and courage can make you do,
But when your sick child cries with shrilling pain,
You left with nothing but pray in vain.

As a mother, we are never sure,
If we want strength for our kid to fight it off,
Or we want peace and serenity to end it all.

Never have I ever been so helpless,
Not sure I want to see my child suffer
Or be childless.

Himshree S
A Mother of a kid who battled Cancer.

PINWHEEL

<u>NILAY SHAH</u>

QUOTE 1:

Open your heart,
Trade the pain.
I can be enough;
for the love that you crave.

QUOTE 2:

I wanted to last.
But I was sand;
in her hand.

<u>VIKAS SONI</u>

THE FAILURE BOY

I am not a lawyer but want to fight for my parents till last
breath
I am not handsome but wants to make my parents happy
I am not a psychologist but wants to know every problem of
my parents
I am not a doctor but wants my parents to feel them fine every
time
I am not a chef but wants to make delicious food every
morning for them
I am a love failure but wants to love them more and more.

PINWHEEL

<u>VANSHIKA SINGH</u>

QUOTE 1:

just be the love you never had &
see the magic happening to the
world in a most beautiful way.

QUOTE 2:

I am ready to walk through the darkness,
if you promise to be the light again.

PINWHEEL

GEETIKA G LABBA

I know men who can make me laugh,
When I am upset and about to quit.
I know men with whom I feel safe,
At unknown places or alone late night.
I know men who are there for me,
When everything seems upside down.
I know who will never let me fall,
The distance between is just a call.
I know men those who will never let me cry.
I know men who can help me to achieve my goals,
Who can act as fuel to my fire.
I know men who can be my support system,
Who can make my day just by their presence.
They are always there for me,
Whenever my spirit needs a lift,
I cannot even thank you for that,
For me you all are truly an extraordinary gift.

PINWHEEL

<u>SHIVI GARG</u>

What if we could be still in our childhood,
Walking on streets, hiding behind wood!

What if we could still ride children train,
Swimming with paper boats in drain!

What if we could still watch peaceful star shine,
Wishing cartoons be mine!

What if we could still enjoy non-stop weeping,
Shouting as if volcano bursting!

What if we could still be in kinder garden,
Carrying small bags as our only burden!

What if we could still do whatever we did
What if we could still be a kid!

SANJALI AGRAWAL

HER OWN

Some loved her,
For her kindness,
Other loved her,
For her warm-heartedness,

Some of them hate her,
For her foolishness,
Other hate her,
For her Possessiveness,

But Deep Down,
She knows,
That no one was her own!

PINWHEEL

<u>TANISH PAL</u>

Give me your hand.
Let's dance, we're in love.
The moon is shining dim at our favourite time.
Let's dance, it'll gonna be war out there.
There are people with bullets behind the door.
Let's dance, the music has stopped...
I can hear your heartbeat from the sky.
Let's dance to the fullest, I can feel your last breath on my
eyes.
You look tired of breathing, let it go.
We were dancing in a cellar door...
Lucky you.

PINWHEEL

<u>CHINMAYANANDA DAS</u>

QUOTE 1:

Dried leaves crumbled under my feet
Beneath the dark open sky
Looked over by countless stars
To take over my silent dance.

QUOTE 2:

Every time I play the audio message
And hear her voice, I smile, innately.
Is it Love or just Friendship?
Or is she just a memory?

PINWHEEL

URVASHI NISHAD

QUOTE 1:

Even life is "temporary" then, why we choose "permanent" things?

QUOTE 2:

"in our life"
We shouldn't wish for anything and it's the way by which we can achieve everything.

ASTHA YADAV

SHOOTING STAR

Sitting alone under the night sky,
She saw a shooting star passing from nearby.
As she moved towards the star,
It started moving far and far.
Soon it landed on the ground,
And started moving there around.
She realised soon that it's a surprise,
God has sent for her in disguise.
Then that star started being unfurled,
To show her the beautiful colours of the world.

PINWHEEL

<u>UTKARSH</u>

QUOTE 1:

Life is tough,
so are you!
remember this dear,
you rock too.

QUOTE 2:
Love isn't something,
and it's not everything.
but it's the very thing,
that makes everything something.

<u>IMRAN ABBAS SABOOWALLA PEN NAME
I.A.S</u>

The drenched melancholy of my soul, might make you feel
little bad,
I cursed the nights so cruelly, my days got scared and sad.
I wish, I wish, I wish,
A wish, I wish came true,
Oo smile and face the darkness, and one day you'll be
through.
-Words of wisdom
I.A.S

QUOTE:

Fear comes from Expectations, then follows Insecurities.
Strength comes from Acceptance, and then follows
Possibilities!
-Words of wisdom
I.A.S

PINWHEEL

JADHAV SHARDA

You taste like
purest form of honey
Natural and smooth
I would wipe it
through my lips whole of it.

Keep your fingers
Playing
She likes them
Over her

PINWHEEL

<u>DEEPIKA KATHIRESAN</u>

QUOTE 1:

If words had wings,
they would have flown long back and
 reached the person I wanted to convey my message to.

QUOTE 2:

When I take some time to relax and close my eyes
Your picture gets portrayed in front though it's for a minute I
rest myself.

PINWHEEL

<u>VAISHNAVI KATTI</u>

WISH YOU WERE HERE
Wish you were here to guide me through all probs
Wish you were here to lend me your soothing arms to solace
Wish you were here to deter all wrongs
Wish you were here to sing lullaby at dusk
Wish you were here to defend me from chides of dad
Wish you were here to let me play a little more against mom
Wish you were here so I needn't find any other to share my
emotions
Wish you were here so you could spot me grow into
headstrong girl
Wish you were here for I always miss you even so never seen
you existing
An ultimate wish that you could come out of that frame and
fulfil all my wishes for once, just once
Wish you were here...

PINWHEEL

AYESHA SHAIKH

QUOTE 1:

The world is full of endless possibilities,
and it is not about the things you have achieved
Or the number of times you have failed,
your passion, drive and motivation will take you places.

QUOTE 2:

And they do not know how hard it is to be a poet,
it is not a glamorous life that gives you the luxury of
happiness,
being a poet makes you roam the dark alley of your memories,
it makes you remember all of the bad things that have
happened to you.

PINWHEEL

<u>SHIKHA</u>

"YOUR HEART BEATS IN ME"
Lustre of your eyes,
Even the stars gasp,
When you caress my worries,
I breathe your essence,
Simple ways, you reach my soul,
Every time I hold your hand,
A scintillating touch,
Dreams come alive,
The moment when we are one,
I complete myself,
I worship, I love you,
An eternal vow,
I have won you over destiny,
I fall for you always,
Pure bliss you are for me,
I wonder, how, but yes
When I close my eyes,
Your heart beats in me!!

PINWHEEL

DIVYA PRIYA A

The universe made you encounter
Miserable people in your life,
The universe seems to be ruthless,
But, listen
From the bottom of your heart.
The universe wants
You to become a healer
To yourself
And to other helpless souls.
The universe wants
People like you
Who are strong enough
To bear pain,
Yet empathetic enough
Not to inflict the same
To other fellow beings.
~ My dear, you're a precious
possession the universe owns.

<u>SAILEE TIWARI</u>

DARK LOVE
Amidst your thousand lies,
In your hundred shades,
I still was true to you,
With my starry eyes, hopeless smiles,
Only if I knew it was all a glass,
Soon to be like a shattered platform,
Perhaps love always had a price to pay,
The tears came incessantly as I realised,
The touch, the feelings held no backbone,
The myriad lights exist like a meaningless dream,
Your words, your eyes, still reverberate,
The memories haunting my every second,
I still question to my naive heart,
Is it the darkness that I was evading from,
Or is it where I was endlessly falling to.

PINWHEEL

<u>SHEREBANU PAGHDIWALA</u>

Thirsty, on the wrecked ship I carve out a map towards you,
a long journey concluded.

Along with your expired promises,
inside of my heart's pocket

My tangled lose hair ends brushing against my bruised knees.
Just like the river brushing the shore
Back and forth.

In the dark, still thirsty waiting for the ship to break, before I
quench my thirst.
It's time, my heart whispered.
I fall, asleep with the water
inside my lungs
Water all above and below me
& I hallucinate the moment where you smiled in our kiss
right when we danced in rain
that day.

PINWHEEL

UDDIPANA CHOWDHURY

THE AUTUMN'S CALL

The November sky is now leaden grey, hey its autumn in the
doorstep. the wild geese call, heir watchword as they fly to
sunnier shores; Within the wood the ripe nuts clattering fall,
and chattering squirrels gather winter stores.
The sere leaves have a sad and mournful sound, as they
shaken by the dreary Autumn wind,
Hey its autumn in the doorstep.
The dusk falls early, and the slim, young moon
Shines fitfully from out a misty sky;
The chill wind rising whines an eerie tune,
The dark wood echoes to the owlet's cry.

PINWHEEL

SWATI BOSE

QUOTE 1:

If there's afterlife, we will meet again, for I know our souls
can't stay apart.

QUOTE 2:

I knew you too were in love when I saw you looking at her the
way I look at you.

PINWHEEL

POOJA SHROFF

"UNTIL YOU DISAPPEAR"
She came to me like the first flower in winter,
She came to me like the spring of my heart,
On a palish pink night,
I followed the spring leaf following you in the pink
timberland,
When i saw you in the ruby night
My heart walked in the wide night to the Unknown you,
When i saw your burnt heart
I wanted to soothe you,
When i heard your bewitched voice
I wanted to immerse in it forever,
When i saw your twinkly scar
I wanted to seal it in my heart,
Until you fly away,
Until you disappear,
I want you to live in my endless memories.

<u>AMAN PREET THAKUR</u>

WANDERING MIND

Sometimes silently,
in isolation.
When mind travels,
through other dimension.

When weird notions,
hit the mind.
A lot of mysteries,
still to find.

Either truth is true,
Or it is an illusion.
Our own existence,
is a matter of confusion.

On this infinite sheet,
where we are just a dot.
Wandering mind is wondering,
we even exist or not.

PINWHEEL

KIRTIJA MOR

QUOTE 1:

Why consider darkness negative?
The moon and the stars shine and love only in the dark to lose
themselves to the day. I haven't seen something more
beautiful.

QUOTE 2:

With an errant yearning for peace,
There's nature for a beautiful gaze

Heavens in sky, mysteries in depth,
All it pulls you to its trough or crest...

PINWHEEL

VANIKA SABERWAL

QUOTE 1:

Words and Silence has their own impact.
Silence in anger & words in pain
Will not hurt but may heal you...

QUOTE 2:

Conversations are most beautiful thing,
because at the end they stay with you forever. So, talk before
everything goes silent for you...

SUMATHI PALANISAMY

PINWHEEL

Pinwheel relates to our life wheel
In our childhood whenever we see pinwheel, we get more
excited might be even now ...But do really the same
excitement remains?
Obviously no ...life changes as it moves on.
As we grow up excitement get decrease and expectations get
increases...
I still remember in my childhood I cried why it not wheeling,
but after I grown up, I came to know the reality that only
because of wind it is wheeling...
Life is also according to the same pattern
We have to know the reality as few people's in our life are like
wind they keep on pushing us but many are there who stops
the wind not to wheel in our life, but we have to stay strong
like stick which holds the pinwheels ...

PINWHEEL

__AYUDHA KEMBHAVI__

When you are gone
I don't want to see you with her
When you are here
I don't want to be with you

Afraid your stars will match hers
Afraid you'll look better with her
Afraid you won't miss me
Afraid you won't want me

Afraid she'll make you smile
Like I did before
Afraid her you'll touch
Like to me u did before

Most of all afraid she'll etch
Deeper scars then I did
And instead of me
Her you'll make yours

PINWHEEL

<u>ANSHIKA RAJ</u>

QUOTE 1:

Unveil yourself BEAUTIFULLY,
You are MAGICAL within.

QUOTE 2:

Now that you left me,
So, you think it's all over.

No! I'm still here,
Hanging up with our memories.

PINWHEEL

www.ingramcontent.com/pod-product-compliance
Lightning Source LLC
LaVergne TN
LVHW091605170726
843492LV00007B/2262